Broomstick Baby

Nervously, Maud dialled the number and waited, then she heard the receiver being lifted.

"Hello, Maud dear, you're in a bit of trouble I believe."

"Oh yes, Aunt Myfanwy Magic," wept Maud. "Everything is terrible and I'm so, so sorry, and Tracey Sharon *is* a witch and Ethel is a bird and Mabel is a hungry cat and Mabel wants to eat Ethel and Tracey Sharon has done something with my book of spells."

Ann Jungman

Broomstick Baby

Illustrated by Lynne Chapman

For Daniel, Tom and Katie

Scholastic Children's Books,
Commonwealth House, 1-19 New Oxford Street,
London WC1A 1NU, UK
a division of Scholastic Ltd
London ~ New York ~ Toronto ~ Sydney ~ Auckland
Mexico City ~ New Delhi ~ Hong Kong

Published in the UK by Scholastic Ltd, 1999

Text copyright © Ann Jungman, 1999
Illustrations copyright © Lynne Chapman, 1999

ISBN 0 439 01135 3

Printed by Cox & Wyman Ltd, Reading, Berks.

2 4 6 8 10 9 7 5 3 1

Chapter 1

Fame at Last

"Look!" yelled Ethel, shaking her sister. "Mabel, will you just look at this!"

Mabel turned over in her sleep and mumbled, "Go 'way. Leave me 'lone," and began to snore again.

"No, wake up," insisted Ethel excitedly. "We're all over the local paper – look at the headlines. 'LOCAL WITCHES FORM BROOMSTICK RESCUES'."

Mabel sat up instantly and snatched the paper from her sister. "Where? Show me."

"There, silly. Right on the front page."

"Well," smiled Mabel. "Isn't that wonderful? An article about us on the front page of the *Plonkford Gazette*, photo and all."

"Don't think much of the picture," grumbled Ethel. "It makes me look as if I've got a squint."

"Never mind," said her sister. "It's all good publicity."

"Why don't I go and put the kettle on while you get dressed," suggested Ethel, "and I'll make us a proper fried breakfast to celebrate?"

"Fantastic!" yelled Mabel, jumping out of bed. "And don't forget three slices of fried bread for me…"

Ten minutes later the two witches sat eating their breakfast, while Mabel read the article out loud. "'For the people of Plonkford witches hold no horrors. We are used to them and we know that far from being the fiends of fairy tales they are a thoroughly good thing. Two years ago Mabel and Ethel came to live in The Towers and began their wonderful gift to the community: putting their broomsticks to good use in BROOMSTICK SERVICES, delivering piping hot food to the windows of one and all—'"

"Ha! That should be good for business," interrupted Ethel.

"'After that,'" continued Mabel, "'our two witch friends started BROOMSTICK REMOVALS, taking to the air to help us move things round the borough quickly and cheaply.'"

"It gets better and better," giggled Ethel.

"'And now,'" continued Mabel, swelling with pride, "'these two amazing women have agreed to help the police, the firemen and the ambulance service in case of emergencies. BROOMSTICK RESCUES are now established as part of Plonkford's emergency services. On behalf of all our readers, a very big thank you to you, Mabel and Ethel.'"

"We're famous!" shouted Ethel, giving her sister a big hug. "Only two years ago we were a pair of witches who didn't know a single human being and now we're famous. Let's go and show Maud. She'll be so proud to see her sisters in the paper."

"She will, she will!" agreed Mabel. "Come on, let's go."

So the two witches jumped on to their broomsticks and flew over to their sister Maud's flat and knocked loudly on her window.

A moment later Maud appeared at the window in her dressing-gown, her hair loose and looking very bad tempered. "What do you two want?" she cried, flinging open the window. "I was just having a really nice lie-in, as befits a pregnant woman."

"Sorry, Maud," mumbled Ethel and Mabel. "We'll go away and leave you to sleep."

"Not much point in that now that you've woken me up," grumbled Maud. "You'd better come in and have some breakfast, unless you've already had some, that is."

"Oh no, Maud, we haven't had any breakfast yet," they lied in unison.

Soon the three sisters were sitting round the kitchen table, drinking steaming mugs of tea, while Mabel proudly read out the piece in the paper...

When Mabel finished, there was a stony silence.

"Well, what do you think, Maud?" asked Ethel nervously.

"Fiddle, faddle," said Maud, sneering. "No mention, I notice, of all the trouble you get into, losing your broomsticks all the time and getting into all kinds of difficulties and going off on holiday and needing to be baled out by me all the time. No, not a mention of your older sister, the one who keeps the show on the road. I'm surprised you have the nerve to show it to me, never mind waking me up to do so."

"Sorry, Maud," sniffed Ethel.

"We didn't think," moaned Mabel apologetically.

"Didn't think! That's your problem, you never do, and then who has to sort out all the consequences? Me, that's who. Well, let me tell you that from now on I am going to be too busy being a mother to bother with you two and don't you forget it."

Just then Maud's husband Fred walked in carrying the paper. "Hello girls," he cried. "Fame at last, eh? And on the front page too. Look at that, Maud."

"Fred, please take that thing away," said Maud icily. "I have seen the paper and am deeply unimpressed. If my sisters wish to disport themselves all over the local paper, I would rather not know about it. In fact, if anyone else says so much as one word about it, I will turn all three of you into rats and good riddance."

"We'll never talk about it again," said Fred soothingly. "Never. Will we, girls?"

The two witches nodded miserably.

"Now, Maud, let me pour you another cup of tea," said her husband. "We don't want you all upset with the baby due so soon."

"Sorry we were so wrapped up in our own thing, Maud," said Mabel. "Any sign of the baby yet?"

"I've been feeling pretty rough for a few days — lots of stomach ache," confessed Maud. "And it's getting worse."

Suddenly Maud doubled up. "In fact, I think I'm going into labour!"

"Maybe we should take her to the hospital!" cried Fred.

"I'll call an ambulance," squeaked Mabel.

"No, a taxi would be better," yelled Ethel.

"No point," replied Fred gloomily. "There's a terrible traffic jam between here and the hospital; it was on the radio."

"Broomstick Rescues to the rescue," smiled Mabel. "Ethel and I will take Maud to the hospital on our broomsticks."

"I am not going on a broomstick in my condition," snapped Maud.

"Of course not, sister dear," agreed Mabel soothingly. "We will tie a sheet tightly to both broomsticks and you and Fred can travel in the sheet. You'll be as snug as a bug in a rug."

"Great idea!" yelled Fred, grabbing two sheets and beginning to tie them to the broomsticks, while Mabel and Ethel threw loads of cushions into the make-shift stretcher.

"We're ready, Maud," Ethel told her. "Come on now, we've put in a whole pile of cushions."

So Fred carefully helped Maud out of the window.

"Come on, off we go!" yelled Mabel.

Soon the four of them were flying off in the direction of the hospital at more than a hundred miles per hour, while down below the traffic was stuck fast in both directions. They landed gently on the hospital lawn right outside the maternity ward, much to the surprise of everyone.

"Good luck, Maud," called Ethel and Mabel, as their sister and her husband pushed open the doors of the ward. "Take care."

"Thanks for the ride," said Maud, turning back for a moment and smiling. "Broomstick Rescues seems to be rather a good thing after all."

Chapter 2

It's a Girl!

"It's a girl!" yelled Fred, and he rushed through the doors and picked up both his sisters-in-law at once and swung them round until all three of them fell over.

Mabel sat up first. "Can we see her? Can we see the baby?"

"Certainly can," smiled Fred. "Come on and meet my daughter."

They went into the ward and there sat Maud, looking much gentler than usual, smiling down at her baby.

"She's gorgeous," breathed Mabel.

"She's the best baby ever," added Ethel.

"Of course she is," agreed Maud.

"What are you going to call her?" asked Mabel. "Merlina, after the great witch?"

"Or Molly, Myfanwy or Morag after the aunts?" suggested Ethel.

"Or even after one of us," added Mabel hopefully.

Maud shuddered. "Oh no, certainly not. Now I have a very important announcement to make, dear sisters, and I want you to listen very carefully. This child is not ever, ever going to be a witch. This child is going to be an absolutely ordinary little girl and no one, absolutely no one is even to mention magic in her presence. Is that absolutely clear?"

"Yes, Maud," chorused the sisters. "No problem with that."

"Good," said Maud, beginning to smile again. "I didn't think you'd take it so well. Now, you may each hold her for just a minute."

So Ethel and Mabel held the baby in turn.

"Goo," said Ethel. "Who's a lovely girl then?"

"Booble, booble, booble," cooed Mabel. "Who's a smasher?"

The baby looked at her aunts and winked.

"Er, Maud," said Mabel. "I hate to say it but I've got a strong feeling this baby is going to have witchy leanings whatever you decide."

"No, sister dear," insisted Maud. "This baby is going to be the most normal and ordinary child in the world. And don't you forget it."

"Well, no child of yours could be that ordinary, Maud," protested Ethel.

"That is true," agreed Maud. "Of course she will be unusually good-looking and clever and sweet natured; that would be normal in a child of mine, as you say, Ethel. But as for witchcraft, I don't ever want to hear the word mentioned anywhere near her."

· The baby let out a big giggle. Maud and Ethel caught each other's eyes but said nothing. "Don't worry, Maud," they assured her. "We faithfully promise that we won't be responsible for your daughter becoming a witch."

"Thank you," cried Maud. "I knew you'd both understand."

"Oh, we understand all right," said Mabel. "Don't worry, Maud, we understand."

As they flew home high over the rooftops, Ethel broke the silence. "What do you make of the baby, Mabel?"

"That baby is the spitting image of the Great Witch Merlina. The spitting image!"

"I know," sighed Ethel. "And that wink and the giggle, all very witchy stuff. Maud won't like it one bit, when she finally realizes."

"She will not," agreed Mabel gloomily.

"And what we have to do is make sure that she can't pin the blame on us. You know what she's like. We'll have to be gooder than good, wear ordinary clothes in front of the baby, never fly around on our broomsticks."

"That's right, and never mention magic or make a spell."

"Or use the word 'cauldron' or discuss flying."

"No, we will have to be very ordinary around that baby, just like any other funny old aunty person."

"It'll be hard," grumbled Mabel.

"It will," agreed her sister. "But better than Maud blaming us for what is about to happen."

"Oh yes," said Mabel, with a shudder. "Maud wouldn't stop at anything; being turned into rats would be mild! We'll just have to be very, very careful."

A few days later Maud came home with the baby.

"No one would ever guess that Maud had once been a witch," whispered Ethel to her sister as Maud, dressed in a short red dress, got out of the car carrying the pretty floral carry-cot. "No more broomsticks for her."

Everyone in the flats turned out to congratulate Maud and Fred and catch a first glimpse of the baby. Maud invited them all up to her flat to have tea and cake. Ethel and Mabel were there helping, both wearing blue jeans and white T-shirts.

"Why aren't you wearing your witchy gear?" asked Jackie, who was the witches' oldest friend and was hoping to be a witch herself one day. "You just don't look right in ordinary clothes."

Maud glowered. Ethel and Mabel grabbed Jackie and dragged her into the kitchen.

"Never use the word 'witch' in front of the baby; Maud is determined that she should grow up not knowing a thing about witchcraft or even that there are witches in the family. So be careful what you say when Maud is around."

"That's daft," protested Jackie. "You are all such good witches and do so many useful things."

"That's as maybe, but Maud has got a bee in her bonnet about it and there's no reasoning with her."

"You'd better believe it," came a little voice.

They all looked down and there sat Rudolfo, Maud's pet rat.

"Oh, hello, Rudolfo," said Mabel. "What's new?"

"What's new is that I'm being thrown out," Rudolfo told them. "Maud says I have to come and live with you, that this is no longer a place for a talking rat."

"I don't want you living with us," said Mabel indignantly. "You're not to be trusted."

"I don't like you much either," sniffed Rudolfo miserably. "But she says we have to live together or she'll turn me into a human and you into rats if there's any fuss."

"Maud is so unreasonable," grumbled Ethel.

"Things are going to be very difficult around here for a while," commented Jackie.

"More than you know," sniffed Mabel. "You see, that is a very witchy baby. Maud is refusing to recognize it but it's as clear as the nose on your face, believe me."

"Oh dear," giggled Jackie. "We're in for some fireworks."

At that moment Maud flung open the kitchen door, her eyes blazing with irritation. "Whatever is going on out here? We need at least fifteen more cups of tea and more cake. Now get on with it."

"Yes Maud, sorry Maud," said Mabel.

As soon as Maud had gone Ethel said: "Jackie, close the door."

Then the two witches raised their arms and chanted:

"Fifteen cups of steaming tea
Be on a tray in front of me.
Fifteen pieces of creamy cake
Ready there for me to take."

And there in front of them was a laden tea tray.

"I'm going to tell on you," shouted Rudolfo with glee.

"No, you're not," Mabel told him, "'cos I know how to turn nasty little telltale rats into people too, and don't you forget it."

"No, Mabel," whimpered Rudolfo. "Sorry, Mabel. Only joking, Mabel."

As Ethel and Mabel served the tea everyone crowded round the baby, who slept through it all…

"What are you going to call her?" people asked.

Maud just smiled mysteriously. "You'll all find out at the christening in a month's time. Everyone is invited. Mabel, will you please ring up the three great-aunts and tell them the news?"

"Shall we invite them to the christening, Maud?" asked Mabel nervously.

"Yes, of course invite them to the christening, but only if they come as ordinary great-aunts. No witchery. Do you understand?"

So Mabel and Ethel had to ring up the three great-aunts – Aunt Morag

McCracken in Scotland, Aunt Molly Murphy in Ireland and Aunt Myfanwy Magic in Wales – and tell them about the baby, about it being a girl, and to come to the christening.

"But Maud doesn't want the baby to know about witches," Mabel told them. "So no witchy clothes, no broomsticks and no magic; we all have to seem ordinary."

"I'm no happy about it," declared Aunt Morag McCracken. "But if that's what yon Maud wants for her wee one, I suppose I'll have to go along with it."

"Well, to be sure that is the biggest load of old hooey I ever heard in all me life, so it is," complained Aunt Molly Murphy. "But sure and all if it's what herself wants, who am I to argue?"

"No witchery!" exclaimed Aunt Myfanwy Magic. "But witchery is such fun; the poor child will be missing out."

"The baby is a witch from the top of her head to the tips of her toes," Mabel told them, "believe me; but none of us must be seen to influence her. We've all got to be very good and ordinary and careful. Maud will have to realize the truth in her own time and her own way. None of us wants to get the blame. Maud is going to be absolutely furious when she finally does find out. Oh dear, I don't like to think about it, really I don't."

Chapter 3

Tracey Sharon

So three weeks later the witches stood in a line in church: Ethel in a blue suit, Mabel in pink, Aunt Myfanwy Magic in grey, Aunt Molly Murphy in green and Aunt Morag McCracken in red – and all wearing hats and gloves and clutching handbags.

Everyone in the neighbourhood had

piled into the church to watch the christening. The vicar stood by the font with Maud holding the baby and Jackie's mum and her gran, who were to be the Godparents.

"I see there are no witches involved," whispered Aunt Morag McCracken sourly. "I'm beginning to regret coming all the way from Scotland for an ordinary, people-type christening."

"Let's just hope it will be ordinary," hissed Mabel, "or there will be no end of trouble."

Everyone in the church went quiet as the vicar began to speak. "In the name of the Father, Son and Holy Ghost, I christen this baby Tracey Sharon."

"Tracey Sharon, that's pretty," mumbled the congregation.

"Tracey Sharon, indeed!" grumbled

Aunt Morag McCracken in disgust. "That's no name for a witch. What can Maud be thinking of?"

At that moment a huge shriek echoed through the church as the vicar poured cold water on to Tracey Sharon's head.

Hastily the vicar handed the baby back to Maud, who kissed her and rocked her backwards and forwards. Gradually a titter began to spread through the congregation and a mutter went up: "Look at the vicar, he's got a huge fish head."

"One of the witches must have done some magic on the vicar."

"What a laugh! I usually find christenings boring but this one's a real giggle."

Maud had gone a deep shade of red and her eyes flashed dangerously. "Take Tracey Sharon out quickly," she whispered fiercely to Fred. "Quick! As fast as you can."

As soon as the baby was out of sight
Maud closed her eyes, raised her arms
and said:

"*Vicar with a head of fish,*
I will do just as you wish.
When I finish, one, two, three,
Once more a human you will be."

Maud opened her eyes and, with a sigh of relief, saw that her spell had worked and that the vicar was back to normal.

"Whatever happened?" gasped the poor man.

"Nothing serious, Vicar," growled Maud. "I am so sorry; it was just some stupid prank and don't worry, whoever did it will be very severely punished, very severely indeed."

"Oh, don't worry yourself about that, my dear Mrs Simpkins," said the vicar cheerfully. "A christening is a joyful occasion; let there only be love and joy on this happy day." And turning to the congregation he said: "Now for our final hymn let us turn to number 247. All together now."

After the service everyone filed over to Maud's for tea and cakes. Mabel and Ethel went straight into the kitchen and began to make tea. Maud came storming in.

"All right, you two, into the bedroom. I've got a few questions to ask. Jackie, you take over in here. I need to have a little chat with my sisters and my great-aunts."

Soon Ethel, Mabel and the three great-aunts were all standing in a line in

Maud's bedroom. "Right!" yelled Maud. "Which one of you was it? Own up now and I won't be too hard on you. Come on, it had to be one of you. No tea or cakes till someone talks."

The five witches stood in a line and said nothing.

"I suppose you're feeling very pleased with yourselves, ruining Tracey Sharon's christening. Was it just one of you who turned the vicar's head into a fish, or all of you? Yes, that's what it will have been, all of you ganging up on poor little me. Well, expect no mercy from me; you were warned and now it's rat time:

"By toad in ditch and owl in tree,
Curses on those who challenge me.
Witches you'll no longer be.
Turn into a small rattee.
Rudolfo he will have a friend,
And I won't go right round the bend."

But Maud's spell had no effect. Maud stared at the five witches in horror.

"What did you expect, Maud?" asked gentle Aunt Myfanwy Magic. "We have five sets of magical powers to set against your one and magic used badly is never as powerful as magic used well."

"Well said, Myfanwy," cried Aunt Morag McCracken. "And I'm no used to being spoken to like this, Maud. I'm glad you have a wee daughter but I'm no hanging around where I'm not wanted, and clearly witches are no longer welcome round here. I'll be off and catch the next train right back to Scotland and I'll thank you not to contact me until you've recovered your manners – and your sanity."

"I'm taking meself off too…" declared

Aunt Molly Murphy. "All this fuss, Maud, just to make sure your daughter doesn't even know she comes from a family of witches. You should be ashamed, Maud, so you should. What your poor, dear mother would say if she were still with us, I tremble to think."

"Calm down, Auntie," said Mabel, taking her hand.

"Well, I'll have to catch a plane back to Ireland since it was a strictly 'no broomsticks' christening, and a pretty penny it cost me – and I hate planes!"

"Oh no, Great-Aunts, don't go," cried Mabel and Ethel. "Maud is just a bit upset. She doesn't mean what she says, do you, Maud?"

"Oh, I do!" yelled Maud, her eyes flashing. "And no one is leaving until you tell me which one of you turned the vicar's head into a fish head."

"It was none of us," sighed Aunt Myfanwy Magic. "None of us would do anything so silly and you know that, Maud. You should go and have a word with Tracey Sharon, now she may know something."

"Don't be ridiculous!" shouted Maud. "She's only three weeks and four days old and she's not a witch and that's final."

"But Maud, the vicar's head—"

"I still think it was one of you."

"I cannot stand another moment of this," declared Aunt Myfanwy Magic. "I'm very disappointed in you, Maud, very disappointed indeed."

"Me too," insisted Aunt Morag McCracken as she put on her coat.

"I couldn't disagree with one word either of you say," sniffed Aunt Molly Murphy.

"I'm driving back to Wales, Ethel and Mabel," Aunt Myfanwy Magic told them. "But if I ever come here again, Maud, be warned: I am coming on my broomstick, because you may be ashamed of being a witch, but I am not."

To cries of "Hear, hear" and "Well said" the three aunts stormed out with their noses high in the air.

Chapter 4

Witchery!

A few days after the christening and the departure of all the great-aunts, Ethel and Mabel sat by the phone waiting for orders for Broomstick Services and reading the paper.

"Anything in the paper about the christening?" asked Ethel.

"No, nothing," Mabel assured her.

"But just listen to this, Ethel. Plonkford Council has announced plans to sell the children's playground to Grabbit, Grabbit and Snatch Ltd, for a development of ten luxury flats."

"They can't do that!" exclaimed Ethel. "Where would the children play?"

"Quite," agreed Mabel. "And now that we're aunts we've got to take that sort of thing seriously."

"I know," sighed Ethel gloomily. "But there's nothing we can do about it."

"You're a wimp, Ethel!" exclaimed Mabel. "I'm surprised at you; there's lots we can do about it."

"Like what?" demanded Ethel.

"Like getting up a petition and going all over the flats getting everyone to sign it."

"That's a good idea," said Ethel,

brightening up. "We could take the petition when we go delivering food or even when we go and rescue someone."

"Ha!" cried Mabel, grinning. "We could call it Broomstick Petitions."

"And," agreed Ethel, warming to the subject, "we could take loads of people to protest outside the Town Hall. We could take them on our broomsticks and call it Broomstick Protests."

"Yes, and we could get everyone to write to the papers and call it Broomstick Letters," added Mabel.

"And we could go and give talks in the schools and get all the children to help," agreed her sister.

"Do you think that if we do all that Maud will speak to us again?"

"Don't know," replied Ethel. "But it's not fair, we've waited all this time to become aunties and now we can't even see little Tracey Sharon."

"It's not fair," agreed Mabel. "I mean, it's not as though any of us did anything."

"That doesn't stop her," groaned Rudolfo, who had suddenly woken up. "Your sister Maud has just got a mean disposition. Serve her right if her daughter is the witchiest witch of the lot. Hee, hee."

"I really do miss Tracey Sharon," said Mabel wistfully.

"Me too," sighed Ethel.

Just then the phone rang. Mabel grabbed it. "Broomstick Services at your service."

"It's Maud here. Fred and I are hungry and would like you to get us something to eat."

"Certainly, Maud. With pleasure, Maud," cried Mabel, grinning at Ethel and giving the thumbs-up sign. "What would you like us to get you?"

"Fish and chips for Fred and a chicken korma for me; but Mabel, please bring it up in the lift. No broomsticks. We don't want Tracey Sharon getting any silly ideas."

"No, Maud. I mean, yes, Maud. Can Ethel come with me? We're both dying to see Tracey Sharon."

"Well, all right, just this once, but no nonsense, not even a hint of it."

"You look after the phone, Rudolfo," shouted the sisters, and Mabel grabbed a piece of paper for the petition as they raced out of the door.

Ten minutes later they were knocking on Maud's door, clasping the piping hot food. "Here you are, Maud," they cried, pushing the food into her hands. "Now where's the baby?"

Tracey Sharon was lying on a rug in front of the fire and gurgling. Ethel went over to her and said: "Hello, poppet."

Tracey Sharon kicked her legs in the air and Ethel disappeared.

"What have you done with poor Ethel?" Maud yelled at Mabel. "I thought I had made it clear I wanted no magic in here."

"I didn't do a thing, Maud," said Mabel tearfully. "And I don't know where poor Ethel is any more than you do."

Just then they heard a bird twittering. They looked up and there high up on the curtains sat a yellow canary.

"We don't have a canary, do we, Maud dear?" asked Fred. "It must have escaped from somewhere and flown in."

"No!" shouted Maud. "That bird's my sister, Ethel. Now, Mabel, turn her back this instant or it will be the worse for you."

"Honestly, Maud…" Mabel began to say, but at that moment Tracey Sharon clapped her hands and Mabel disappeared too. A moment later a large tabby cat stood on the rug next to the baby.

"Is that Mabel?" asked Fred nervously.

"It looks like it," moaned Maud. "Oh Fred, what are we going to do? I can't bear it; Tracey Sharon must have witchy powers after all. Oh, this is all my fault because I was so blind and stupid. I'm sorry, Fred, so very sorry. I did want our daughter to be completely ordinary."

"I didn't," said Fred cheerfully. "I like witches myself. In fact, I'm thrilled to bits that our daughter is a witch."

At that moment the cat that had been Mabel let out a howl and tried to climb the curtain. The bird that had been Ethel squeaked and flew to the highest point in the room.

Fred turned white. "You've got to do something, Maud. You still remember all your magic from the old days. Come on, do something before it is too late and Mabel eats Ethel."

"Get my book of spells! I hid it underneath all the saucepans."

"It's not there," cried Fred, desperately throwing all the saucepans on the floor.

"Tracey Sharon, what have you done with my book of spells? Please tell me or Auntie Mabel will eat your Auntie Ethel."

"Ugg," said Tracey Sharon and put her toe in her mouth.

"The great-aunts," groaned Maud. "I'll have to phone them and apologize and eat humble pie. Oh, why have I been so blind and stupid? Mabel will eat Ethel and it will all be my fault."

"Try Myfanwy first," suggested Fred. "She's so sweet and kind, she'll forgive you if you explain."

Nervously, Maud dialled the number and waited, then she heard the receiver being lifted.

"Hello, Maud dear, you're in a bit of trouble I believe."

"Oh yes, Aunt Myfanwy Magic," wept Maud. "Everything is terrible and I'm so, so sorry, and Tracey Sharon *is* a witch and Ethel is a bird and Mabel is a hungry cat and Mabel wants to eat Ethel and Tracey Sharon has done something with my book of spells."

"Oh dear," sighed Aunt Myfanwy Magic. "I knew something was wrong, I could see it in my crystal ball, but this is serious. Let me see. Well, first of all give Mabel some fish, so she isn't chasing Ethel for a bit."

"Quick, Fred, give Mabel your fish," commanded Maud. "She's eating the fish, Auntie. Now, what next?"

"I'm looking in my book of spells. Let's
see, try this:

> "I, your mother, say to you,
> All your naughty deeds undo.
> I will treat you as a witch
> If these wicked spells you ditch."

Fred and Maud stared at Tracey Sharon,
who blew bubbles and said: "Ugg, goo."
Fred and Maud held their breath.

"What's happening?" asked Myfanwy down the phone.

"Oh Auntie, nothing," wept Maud.

"Pick the baby up and say it again in a stern voice," suggested the Welsh witch.

Maud picked Tracey Sharon up and, looking her in the eyes, repeated the spell in an angry voice.

"Oh, all right, Mum. You win," said Tracey Sharon to her parents' amazement, and then she sneezed loudly. Suddenly, there in front of them stood Mabel and Ethel.

"It's all right this end, Myfanwy," Fred shouted down the phone. "Thanks so much. Byeee."

Maud handed Tracey Sharon to Fred and flung her arms round her sisters. "Oh Ethel, Mabel, I'm so happy to see you and I'm so sorry that I didn't listen to you and the great-aunts. I'll never doubt you again or boss you around or be rude and I'm so glad you got an article in the paper all to yourselves. Please forgive me."

"Of course, Maud," said the sisters. "But for what? What happened?"

"Well, it turns out that Tracey Sharon really *is* a witch and the naughty creature turned you into a canary, Ethel, and Mabel into a hungry cat. If Aunt Myfanwy Magic hadn't known what to do you'd probably be in Mabel's tummy by now, Ethel."

Mabel and Ethel looked at their niece, who was happily cooing and smiling on her rug.

"Oh dear," commented Mabel. "I can see that we are going to have to do something about that young lady."

"You'd better believe it, Auntie," said Tracey Sharon with a giggle. "You'd just better believe it!"

Chapter 5

Little Miss Super-Witch

"Oh no!" groaned Rudolfo, when Ethel and Mabel told him what had happened. "This is terrible news."

"What's so bad about it?" demanded Mabel. "We've got another witch in the family. I think it's terrific."

"For you maybe," whimpered the rat. "This new witch may be another one who wants to turn me into a human-type person."

"On the other hand," Ethel pointed out, "she may have even stronger magic than her mother and be able to stop Maud turning you into a human being."

Rudolfo grinned from ear to ear. "Now, that is a good thought. Would you ask Tracey Sharon to make sure that I am always a rat?"

"What will you do for us if we do?"

"I will promise never to rat on you again. I will be a rat who doesn't rat."

"You're on," Mabel told him. "Leave it with us."

Just then there was a knock on the window and there on her broomstick sat Maud with Tracey Sharon sitting behind her, clinging on to her mother.

"Sorry to bother you," said Maud in

her most polite voice, "but I was wondering if you could look after Tracey Sharon while Fred and I go to see the vicar?"

"It would be a pleasure, Maud," said the sisters together, smiling at Tracey Sharon.

"Thank you, Auntie Mabel. Thank you, Auntie Ethel," said Tracey Sharon, and she put out her arms for Mabel to help her in through the window.

"I can't get over how well you talk for a five-week-old," commented Ethel.

"It is because I am a superwitch, Auntie Ethel. Superwitches are born knowing," Tracey Sharon told her, as Maud laid her down in front of the fire. "I was able to talk from day one but I decided not to tell anyone at first. You did all sound silly saying, 'goo' and 'boo' and 'gaa' at me."

"Don't be rude," Maud told her daughter. "And be very good and do everything your aunts tell you while your father and I arrange a new christening."

"A new christening?" questioned Mabel.

"Well, yes, of course," snapped Maud. "Are you soft in the head or something, Mabel? I don't know why I had to be cursed with such dozy sisters. Now that we know that Trace— my daughter is a superwitch, she must have a more suitable witchy name. I would have thought that was obvious."

"You sound more like your old self, Maud," commented Mabel cheerfully.

"Well, you'd try the patience of a saint," grumbled Maud. "Now you behave, all of you, and that includes you, Rudolfo. Don't think I can't see you skulking in the corner there, you little rat."

"Yes, Maud. Hello, Maud," whispered Rudolfo.

"I'll be back in an hour or so and no nonsense while I'm away, is that clear?"

"Yes, Maud," chorused Ethel, Mabel and Rudolfo.

"Yes, Mummy," called Tracey Sharon.

As Maud flew off, Mabel smiled at her niece. "OK, kiddo, now let's see what you can really do. Let's find out if you really are a superwitch."

"What would you like me to do?" asked Tracey Sharon. "I could turn you into frogs or turn the water green or make Rudolfo fly."

"Easy, peasy," sneered Mabel. "No, I want you to show me that you have stronger magic than your mother. Put a spell on Rudolfo, so that even if Maud tries she can't turn him into a person."

Tracey Sharon laughed, "Really, Auntie, that is too easy. All right, here goes:

Rudolfo is a nasty rat,
And he must be content with that.
He cannot a person be,
Particularly by my mummy."

Ethel and Mabel clapped enthusiastically.

"Sounds good, kiddo," said Mabel. "Now let's test if it works. Ethel, come over here and we'll both try and turn Rudolfo into a human. Our joint witch power is about the same as Maud's."

Rudolfo cowered in a corner, shaking, and covered his eyes.

"By toad in ditch
And owl in tree,
This rat must now a human be,
In the count of one, two, three."

"I'm still a rat!" shrieked Rudolfo, bursting into tears. "Oh thank you, Tracey Sharon, you are my best friend in the whole world. I'm so happy, so very, very happy."

"Well," commented Ethel, "so you really are a superwitch."

"That's right," smiled Tracey Sharon.

"Fancy having a superwitch for a niece," said Mabel proudly. "I won't know what to do with you; you'll be better at magic than any of us."

"I'll be very good, especially for you, Auntie Mabel," said the baby superwitch sweetly.

"So what do you want to do?" asked Mabel nervously. "We could bake a cake or go for a walk or play with building bricks, or go and join in the demonstration against building houses on the children's playground."

"Boring," grumbled the baby superwitch.

"What then?" demanded Mabel. "You're not practising any spells if that's what you're thinking of."

"Of course not," agreed Tracey Sharon. "But I do want to practise broomstick flying. A witch needs to be good at that, particularly a superwitch."

"Only indoors," declared Ethel and she firmly locked all the windows.

"Oh, all right," grumbled Tracey Sharon. "If you say so."

So Mabel flew round the flat with Tracey Sharon sitting cosily in front of her aunt. Tracey Sharon shrieked with delight.

"Can I have a go on my own?" she asked. "Oh please, Auntie Mabel, nice Auntie Mabel?"

"Can I trust you?" growled Mabel.

"Oh yes, Auntie, you certainly can, Auntie Mabel. Just in the flat, I promise faithfully."

"Oh, give the girl a go, you old spoilsports," interrupted Rudolfo. "She's all right, a definite improvement on her mother."

"She didn't turn *you* into a cat," muttered Mabel, as she handed the broom over to Tracey Sharon.

The baby flew round the room a couple of times, banging into walls and nearly sliding off, then she began to get the hang of it.

"Look at me!" she cried. "I'm a super-duper superwitch." And then with a

swoop she flew right up the chimney.

"Ethel, Tracey Sharon has flown up the chimney!" yelled Mabel. "Oh, why did I listen to Rudolfo?"

"She won't be able to get out," Ethel assured her sister. "The chimney is blocked off higher up."

Mabel stuck her head up the chimney. "Tracey Sharon, are you all right?"

A lump of soot fell and Ethel heard a little giggle.

"Are you up there, Tracey Sharon, you naughty, naughty girl?"

A heap of soot fell on Mabel's upturned face and she staggered back, coughing.

"She's still up there all right," Ethel told her sister. "But how are we going to persuade her to come down? It sounds as though she's having a good time up there."

"I'll get her down all right," snapped Mabel. "Give me the other broom, Ethel. I'll make it so uncomfortable for her, she'll be begging to come down."

"No!" protested Rudolfo. "You're behaving like a rat, Mabel. That's your little niece up there."

"If you're so sympathetic, you go and get her out," shouted Mabel.

"All right, I will, but only if you make sure Maud knows exactly who it was who rescued her daughter."

"It's a deal," agreed Mabel.

"And if I don't come back remember only the nice things about me."

"Not many of those," mumbled Mabel. "Rudolfo, you stand on my broomstick and I'll push it up the chimney.

Gingerly Rudolfo did as she said.

"Oh, oh!" he squeaked. "It's so dark and dirty up here, I feel really at home."

"Have you found her yet?" yelled Ethel.

"She's here and she's stuck," called Rudolfo.

"Hurry up," shouted Mabel. "Maud's coming. I can see her walking across the gardens. Hurry up."

"Get her unstuck and fast," called Ethel desperately. "Maud's coming back."

"The broomstick is stuck. I'll have to nibble my way through it," replied the rat.

"Well, nibble fast, very fast," Ethel told him.

The two witches stood by the fireplace and listened. They could hear the sound of Rudolfo busily nibbling and Tracey Sharon cheerfully encouraging him. Then suddenly Rudolfo and Tracey

Sharon fell out of the fireplace, followed by the broken broom, spreading soot everywhere. At that very moment Maud walked in.

"Whatever is going on?" she demanded fiercely. "Can't I even leave your niece here for two minutes without something terrible happening? Come to Mummy, darling," she cooed at Tracey Sharon, who with a wicked grin flung her arms round her mother.

"Huh! Well, now we're all covered with soot," commented Mabel. "And it's all Tracey Sharon's fault."

"That's right, always blame someone else, you mangy cowards, you."

"Oh, it is my fault, Mummy, really it is," Tracey Sharon told her proudly. "I flew up the chimney for fun and got stuck and Rudolfo rescued me."

Maud gritted her teeth but managed to say: "Thank you, Rudolfo."

Rudolfo grinned and his chest swelled with pride. "Think nothing of it, Maud," he said casually. "Anything for you any time, you know that."

"You can come to the new christening in six weeks' time," Maud told him. "And

this time there will be no nonsense."
And grabbing her child and her broom
she flung open the window and flew off.

"No nonsense indeed!" sniffed Ethel.
"She'll be lucky."

"Quite," agreed Mabel. "She must be
joking. Little Miss Superwitch will get
up to some kind of mischief and that's
a fact."

"Oh yes, she will," giggled Rudolfo
gleefully. "She's my girl and she'll cause
no end of trouble."

Ethel + Mabel Witch
No. 176 The Towers
Plonkford

Chapter 6

Merlina

"Let me open it," cried Mabel, grabbing the large white envelope sitting on the kitchen table.

"No, me," shrieked Ethel, trying to take it from her sister.

"I'll open the envelope and then you pull it out," suggested Mabel.

"All right," agreed Ethel. "Only hurry

up, I'm dead curious. No one ever writes to us."

So Mabel tore the envelope open and Ethel pulled the contents out of the envelope and together they read:

> *Mr and Mrs Fred Smith request the*
> *pleasure of the company of*
> ## *Ethel and Mabel*
> *at the rechristening of their*
> *daughter, Tracey Sharon,*
> *at St Bride's Church, Plonkford*
> *Green on Sat. March 31st.*
> *This unusual event is due to*
> *unforeseen circumstances.*
> *Second presents are not expected.*
> *R.S.V.P. Maud or Fred.*

"We'll have to go," commented Mabel. "I mean, anything could happen."

"Definitely," agreed her sister. "That little superwitch could get up to terrible mischief if last time is anything to go by."

"Yes, and we'd better get the great-aunts there – our combined magic may just be too much for that Tracey Sharon."

"We'd better ring the great-aunts, I suppose," said Ethel glumly.

"Bagsy you phone Aunt Morag McCracken," cried Mabel quickly. "I bet she's still in a terrible mood after the last christening."

"I know," sighed Ethel. "And you can hardly blame her after the way Maud behaved."

"Well, you'll just have to explain how serious the situation is and that the reputation of all witches is at stake."

So, nervously, Ethel picked up the phone and told Aunt Morag what had happened.

"I'm no coming unless yon Maud apologizes to me," snapped Aunt Morag fiercely. "Not in all my born centuries has anyone ever spoken to me like that."

"Oh please, Auntie Morag, anything could happen. Please put your pride aside. Having a superwitch in the family is no joke. We really need your help to control Tracey Sharon. Mother would have wanted you to come."

"Aye, she would that. Well, I'll come to help you and Mabel for your dear mother's memory, but this time I'm brooming in and wearing my usual clothes."

"That's wonderful, Auntie. Thank you so much. See you on March 31st and have a nice fly down."

After that, Mabel rang Aunt Mollie Murphy and after four hours of persuading she agreed to come too. Aunt Myfanwy had already spoken to Maud and was flying in a few days before the christening to look after the magic side of things.

However, something happened that put all thoughts of the christening out of everyone's heads. A notice appeared on the entrance to the children's playground. It read:

 # KEEP OUT!
THIS PLAYGROUND IS CLOSED.
THIS LAND IS NOW OWNED BY GRABBIT, GRABBIT AND SNATCH LTD.
TRESPASSERS WILL BE PROSECUTED.

The children all started to cry loudly.

"I want to play on the swings," yelled one.

"Why can't I go on the slide?" sniffed another.

"We want our playground back," cried a group of others.

"No need to panic," Maud told the children and parents. "We'll just ignore their silly notice and keep a twenty-four-hour guard here. Then, if they try and send in the bulldozers, we can lie down and stop them."

So a rota was drawn up and all night two locals guarded the playground and life went back to normal, and by the time the christening came round they had all stopped worrying about the playground.

So on the appointed Saturday the five witches sat in Ethel and Mabel's kitchen making plans.

"I think we should all stand in a row at the christening and hold hands,"

said Aunt Myfanwy Magic, "just in case young Tracey Sharon tries any nonsense again; our joint magic could put it right."

"Aye, indeed," said Aunt Morag McCracken. "Better safe than sorry."

"And I've brought some lucky shamrock with me from Ireland," added Aunt Molly Murphy. "Every little thing helps. Here's a bit for everyone; put it in your pockets, my darlings."

"Ethel and I have made some of the special brew that is drunk before the christening of a superwitch," Mabel told them. "Ethel, pour some into each cup and then we must recite *The Great Witch's Hymn* for times of special danger!"

So they stood in a circle with the cups of bubbling brew held high in the air and spoke the famous anthem:

"Solemn circle, solemn form,
We the witches come to warn.
No one must our spells deny,
For we are greater than the sky.
Superwitch so young and bold,
You who will not be told,
To our wisdom you must bend,
To join our power in the end."

 "Oh pooh!" sniffed Rudolfo. "What a lot of old nonsense. My Tracey Sharon is much more powerful than you silly old bats."

Aunt Morag McCracken fixed Rudolfo with her beady eye. "I'm tempted, laddie, very tempted to turn you into a human being. Och yes, I really am."

"Sure, and if we were all to say the spell together," cried Aunt Molly Murphy, "I've no doubt it would work, whatever baby superwitch has done."

"Sorry," yelled Rudolfo. "It was only my little joke. Honestly, a rat can't make a joke round here any more. Where's your sense of humour? I think this christening is getting to you all."

"All right, I'll no do it this time," said

Aunt Morag McCracken. "But you mind your manners, my wee rat, or it will be the worse for you."

"It's time to go," Ethel reminded them. "We don't want to be late."

"Mount broomsticks," cried Mabel. "One, two, three, go!" And out of the window they flew in convoy.

Soon they were sitting in a line in the front row of the church. Behind them sat everyone else muttering away.

"I wonder what that child will do today," said one person.

"Whatever it is it won't be good," commented another.

"She's a shocker that one," said someone else. "Nothing but trouble in my view."

The witches looked at each other and clasped hands grimly.

This time the curate was doing the christening; the vicar had gone off sick at the very last minute.

"I expect he was scared of a repeat of last time," whispered Ethel.

Everyone nodded in agreement.

But this time the ceremony went off without anything out of the ordinary happening. The baby didn't cry, not even when the curate poured cold water on her and said: "I christen you Merlina Tracey Sharon."

"Maybe she's a reformed character," whispered Mabel.

"No!" hissed Aunt Myfanwy Magic. "It's because our magic is too strong; I can feel it in my finger tips. We can't relax until the christening is completely over."

Soon the witches were over in the church hall with everyone else and began to tuck into some of the delicious food they had helped prepare. Everyone in the flats was there and they had agreed to relax the guard on the playground for the occasion, so that every last adult and child could join in the fun. Maud made a little speech about why they had needed a second christening and Fred told everyone how happy he was that his daughter was a witch.

Suddenly Merlina Tracey Sharon

piped up: "I've got something I want to say at my very own christening."

Everyone was very surprised. "She's much too young to be talking," they whispered.

"Hello everyone," cried the superwitch. "Particularly all the boys and girls out there. I think this silly old tea is

dead boring and I want to offer you all a broomstick ride. Everyone, grab one of the witches' broomsticks lying around and when I say 'Shabang' they'll become airborne. Grab a cake or something and we can pelt them down there."

The adults stared in horror and went to grab their children, but too late!

"Shabang!" yelled Merlina Tracey Sharon. Within a minute the children were flying round the hall, chucking sandwiches and cakes, sausage rolls, ice-cream, tea and coffee, wine and champagne at the unfortunate adults below. Ethel, Mabel and the three great-aunts rushed into a corner, closed their eyes and held hands.

"Let me join in," they heard Maud shout. "You need my magic too." So they let Maud join the circle and chanted:

*"Superwitch, so young and out of hand,
One, two, three and you will land."*

Within a second all the broomsticks flew to the ground and the surprised children fell off. The witches grabbed their broomsticks hurriedly and the parents grabbed their children.

Maud caught hold of Merlina Tracey Sharon. "You naughty, naughty girl!" Maud shouted.

"Well, honestly, Mum, what did you expect me to do?" grinned Merlina Tracey Sharon. "Christenings are boring."

"You're so ungrateful," began Maud. "Really I—"

"Shush, Mum," said Merlina Tracey Sharon, sitting up straight. "Quiet, everyone."

"What is it?" asked Aunt Myfanwy Magic sharply.

"Bulldozers. Bulldozers moving towards the children's playground."

"How do you know?" demanded Ethel.

"I can see them in my mind – four bulldozers, red and yellow, moving towards the fence of the playground."

"Grabbit, Grabbit and Snatch are playing dirty," declared Maud grimly.

"Yes," agreed everyone. "What a rotten trick."

"They must have heard about the christening and they knew there wouldn't be any guards for an hour or two… Come on, everyone, let's get 'em," shouted the curate.

"Witches, get moving," cried Mabel. "When superwitches see things, something bad is afoot. On to your broomsticks and off we go!"

And all the witches leapt on to their

brooms and flew off in the direction of the playground with the other guests streaming out of the door behind them.

As the witches approached the playground they saw that Merlina Tracey Sharon was right, there were the bulldozers chugging towards it.

"Good girl," said Maud grimly to her daughter. "Now all we have to do is stop them."

"And how are we going to do that?" asked Mabel anxiously.

"I'll turn all the wee men into haggises," said Aunt Morag McCracken fiercely.

"Good idea," laughed Ethel. "But Auntie, be careful you don't harm the people on our side."

"Let's dissolve the bulldozers," suggested Merlina Tracey Sharon, giggling. "If we do that those horrible people will never come back."

"Clever girl," said Mabel approvingly. "If Grabbit, Grabbit and Snatch lose expensive machines, that will really worry them. You're dead right, that is the best plan to keep them away from our playground, once and for all."

"Can you think of a spell?" asked her mother. "One that we could all say together."

"Mmmm," said Merlina Tracey Sharon. "How about:

"*We the witches of this city*
Will show to you no pity.
Bulldozers red and yellow, we say to you,
Turn into a pool of glue.
Our playground you will not destroy,
Higgle, Piggle, Diggle, Doy!"

"It might work if we all say it together," cried Aunt Myfanwy Magic. "Come on, we'll fly in a circle all round them and say the spell three times. One, two, three, all together now."

So the witches swooped down and flew round and round as fast as they could, intoning the spell. The men driving the bulldozers were terrified. Then suddenly at the third "Higgle, Piggle, Diggle, Doy!" all the bulldozers vanished and the drivers found themselves sitting in a pool of glue.

"Don't turn us into frogs please," they cried. "We only work for the company. We think it's a rotten shame turning a playground into luxury flats."

"We'll be nice this time and spare you," Maud told them. "But if you ever come back here again it won't be frogs but haggises for you. My great-aunt Morag McCracken here is just waiting to turn someone into a haggis. Isn't that so, Auntie?"

"Aye, it is that. My fingers are positively itching. I'm having a hard time controlling myself."

"You tell your bosses that and say they are to leave our playground alone," continued Maud. "Now off you go."

Just then all the guests from the christening turned up.

"Where are the bulldozers?" they asked. "Did Merlina Tracey Sharon get it wrong?"

"No way!" cried Merlina Tracey Sharon. "There are the bulldozers; we turned them into little pools of glue and now our playground is safe for ever!"

"Hurray," cried the crowd, as the drivers slunk off.

"Thank goodness for superwitches is all I can say," said Jackie.

"Yes, I think she is going to be a good thing after all," agreed Ethel. "It looked a bit dodgy there for a while, but I think Merlina will be a great help to Broomstick Rescues and all our other enterprises." And all the crowd cheered and cheered.

After that everyone went back into the church hall and ate and drank and danced until late into the night. The witches made sure that no matter how much people ate and drank their glasses were always full and their plates overflowing. The local paper covered the event with loads of photographs and got an interview with Merlina Tracey Sharon.

The next week Ethel and Mabel poured over their copy of the *Plonkford Gazette*. They were delighted to see a picture on the front page of Fred and Maud with Merlina Tracey Sharon and Rudolfo at their feet.

"Just look at that headline," cried Ethel. "'PLONKFORD WELCOMES THE BIRTH OF A SUPERWITCH.'"

"Read it out to me," squeaked Mabel.

PLONKFORD

GAZETTE

PLONKFORD WELCOMES THE BIRTH OF A SUPERWITCH.

"'On behalf of the people of Plonkford this paper would like to welcome Merlina Tracey Sharon into our community, and would like to thank her parents, Fred and Maud, for choosing to live in Plonkford. Long may the superwitch who saved our children's playground live in our midst.'"

"That should please Maud," commented Mabel. "She didn't like it one bit when we had a mention in the paper and she was left out."

Just then there was a knock at the window. Ethel went and opened it. There hovered Maud with Merlina Tracey Sharon sitting behind and Rudolfo behind her.

"Morning, sisters," said Maud cheerfully. "Just thought I'd drop in and cheer you up with the local paper."

"Anything interesting in it, Maud?" asked Ethel, grinning.

"Yes, anything we should know about?" added Mabel.

"Oh, no," said their sister, trying to sound casual. "Just thought that you might like to know that all the family have now made it into the *Plonkford Gazette*. And I mean to say, Merlina is only a few weeks old. Unlike some I could name but won't." And she flew off calling over her shoulder: "Byee, sisters."

"Byee, sillies," smirked Rudolfo.

"Byee, Aunties," cooed Merlina Tracey Sharon, waving and smiling sweetly.

The End